Splintered Dreams

Dare to Love Book Series
Book 1

Diana Lynn

D & D Graphics
Castro Valley, CA

Diana Lynn/D & D Graphics
Castro Valley, CA/94546
http://dianalynnwrites.com

Publisher's Note: This is a work of fiction. Names, characters, places, and incidents are a product of the author's imagination. Locales and public names are sometimes used for atmospheric purposes. Any resemblance to actual people, living or dead, or to businesses, companies, events, institutions, or locales is completely coincidental.

Any questions, comments, or media inquiries please email: mailto: mailto:info@dianalynnwrites.com

Book Layout © 2017 BookDesignTemplates.com

Splintered Dreams/ Diana Lynn. — 1st ed.
ISBN 978-1-947594-95-1

There are so many to thank, but most of all I thank my family for their support; Don, Brian and Jeff.

Daring to love is the courage to love ourselves and risk disappointment. Be loving. Be Brave. Be Strong. Be compassionate.

–DIANA

Chapter One

Crisa

S oft jersey sheets tangled around my naked body as I rolled over and stared at the dated popcorn ceiling. I'd vowed to replace it countless times, but could never quite find the time to actually do it.

"Wow."

My eyes traced the defined ridges of the ceiling as I tallied the bumps, grateful I'd been too lazy to scrape the ceiling.

A hand snaked under the covers to intertwine with my fingers, and a massive arm draped over my belly.

"That good, huh?"

Pride radiated from the deep, gravelly voice that rasped in my ear.

"Oh, yeah," I turned my face so he wouldn't see the effort I put into making the lie believable.

As his arm tightened around me, pulling my curves against the hard angles of his body, my eyes fell on the small photograph perched atop my nightstand. The faces were as familiar to me as my own reflection, but the youthful, glowing wedding couple in the center were now strangers. Time, children, and life had sown thin lines in the corners of my eyes and strands of gray in my chestnut hair. I'd traded in the wedding-day hopefulness for realistic cynicism, and dreams of traveling the world and ending global hunger became goals of paying off my car and waiting until sunset for a glass of wine.

In the photo, I had been Mrs. Alan Brant. I was still Mrs. Alan Brant, but everything else had changed, the most recent evidence of which was the man in my bed.

He wasn't Alan.

"Crisa?" He murmured, his tone confused and concerned.

When I turned to look at him, I had to blink a few times to reassure myself that no, he wasn't Alan.

"Are you all right?"

"Of course!" I replied, forcing a bright smile and injecting chipper confidence into my response. He relaxed and tugged me to him again until I could feel his chest hair tickling my back.

His name was Lawrence Nader, fifty-four, a prominent forensic accountant, a charming gentleman, and lousy in bed. I'd spent the last seventeen minutes trying to remember the pilot episode of *Friends* word-for-word and do my best impression of an opera singer at the end when Lawrence announced he was ready. I had become an expert at faking orgasms during the last several years of our thirty-year marriage, but after my last few sexual encounters I felt confident I could teach a graduate-level course on the topic.

Alan and I hadn't wed with the passionate devotion typical of young love. When I walked down the aisle at the tender age of twenty-one, Alan was fifteen years my senior, worked as a Regional Sales Executive, and drank a bourbon after work every day. He had his flaws, but he loved me and wanted to marry me. I considered myself lucky to find someone who cared for me and told myself I should be content with a man like Alan. He loved me, after all. *Right?*

I abandoned my notions of belly-swooping, heart-stopping romance in favor of sensible affection. Had I known what I learned years later, after the birth of our third and final child at thirty, I may not have foregone my desire to find true love. After his two affairs he gave a heartfelt apology.

Alan then offered me the house, one of the cars, a sizeable alimony check, and a divorce all in one neat little package for his transgressions. I declined. We stayed married for another twenty years. Perhaps I was happiest in the arms of security rather than the arms of a soulmate.

Now, I was in Lawrence's arms. After a disappointing experience I wanted him to leave, but I hadn't worked out a way to nicely kick him out of my bed. My fake orgasm seemed to have convinced him he was some kind of sex god, and now I was stuck with his apparent desire to snuggle. If I'd been a colder person, I might have told him I hated spooning.

I didn't have the heart to tell him he was nestled in the same spot where my husband died of a heart attack seven months ago. Luckily for him, I wasn't so jaded to want everyone else to be miserable with me. No, I would leave him to his ignorant bliss.

Lawrence was the fourth in my line of dates since Alan's passing. After Alan's indiscretions came to light, I told myself I forgave him, but now that I was a single woman, I wasn't sure that was true. I loved my husband despite the lack of fairytale romance, but after a few months of grieving I found myself wanting to understand the thrill of meaningless sex, to learn why Alan compromised the life he'd built with me.

Unfortunately, I didn't have an answer. The men I'd brought back to my bedroom had respectable jobs, good reputations, and decent personalities, but my feelings for them didn't extend beyond friendship, and the bedroom performance was almost mediocre. It was sex without an emotional connection; it wasn't fun. I was a widow with all the freedom in the world, but my loneliness and dissatisfaction trapped me.

I didn't know I'd started to drift off amidst my unhappy musings until Lawrence spoke.

"I suppose I'd better get going," he whispered.

I started rolling on my back, propping myself up on my hands.

"Okay," I would have mustered a tone of false disappointment if I'd been able, but the most I could manage was casual complacency. "Thank you, I had a nice time."

"My pleasure." He leaned over and kissed my forehead before shuffling out of bed. I watched as he dressed, buttoning his pressed shirt up to his neck with care and drawing his trousers over his knees. He was an attractive man, slim for his age and in the early stages of hair loss, but I didn't feel *it*. I couldn't explain what exactly *it* was, but I definitely knew I wasn't getting any closer to figuring it out with Lawrence.

I wasn't sorry to see him go. He deserved someone better, someone who appreciated all of his quirks and characteristics. I doubted I could have ever been *the one* for him.

He draped his sport jacket over his arm, walked to my side of the bed, and kissed me on the forehead again. "I'll call you."

"Great," I murmured as I forced an enthusiastic smile.

He returned it with one of his own and left, his footsteps fading down the hall until I heard the squeak of my front door opening, followed by the bang as it shut behind him. *Hope it didn't hit him on the way out* I thought dryly, before scolding myself for being petty. It wasn't his fault he wasn't what I was looking for. I sighed and flopped back onto the pillows, resigning myself to another lonely night. As my eyes closed, I mentally crossed my fingers that I hadn't missed my chance at true love when I settled with Alan all those years ago. There had to be someone out there for me...*right?*

I needed a hobby. One-night stands and disinterested romantic trysts wouldn't fill the void in my life.

Chapter Two

Slade

Twenty-three years at the same firm, in the same paneled office on the third floor of the same beige-brick building, next to the same dingy bar where I ordered the same Tom Collins every weekday after work. After twenty-three years, you'd think I would have mastered the art of sipping coffee from the black mug I used each morning with *Lawyers Suck!* printed in white on the side.

I hadn't.

The steaming liquid dribbled down my chin before blooming across my shirt like my own personal Rorschach test. I choked in response, and a flood of coffee flew from the mug's mouth and splattered across my desk, pooling and worming its way toward the now-forgotten deposition file on my desk.

"Damn," I cursed and scrambled to find something to clean the mess. My options were limited, so I settled on Post-It notes in the absence of napkins.

The message that led to the whole sloppy debacle was still playing, the sultry voice rolling through my office like an unwelcome tidal wave of drama. I banged my phone with my elbow to turn it off, jarring more coffee from the mug, this time, sending it raining to the carpeted floor. I groaned in frustration. Rebecca always did this to me.

Sopping up enough of the spill to avoid total disaster, I dropped into my chair and glared at the phone. The light indicating a new voicemail continued to flash since I'd only listened to half the message. I didn't want to hear the rest, but I also didn't want that irritating light to blink all day and remind me of her. I considered erasing it, but she had a tendency to show up in the worst places at the most inconvenient times. I needed to know if I should expect another stunt from her. Groaning again, I punched the button and listened.

"I haven't heard from you in a while." Her slow, calculated voice was always dripping with enough sensuality to earn an R-rating, and this time was no different. *"You never seem to have time for me anymore. I know being a lawyer takes up a lot of time, but I miss you. Call me, Slade."*

"Yeah, right," I growled, waiting for the automated female voice to tell me it was the end of the message before I could press delete.

Rebecca was a woman I dated for a short time a few months ago. She was a divorcee in her mid-forties who dressed like she was twenty-two and sought men with money. If I was honest with myself, my interests were primal, and Rebecca was willing to satiate that need. After I bedded her on our first date, she called again. I wasn't the kind of jerk who slept with a woman and then tossed her aside, so I took her on a second date.

As it turns out, I should've been that jerk. What I interpreted as loneliness and a desire for companionship turned out to be a web of intricate manipulations woven to justify her hyper-clingy obsession and desire to advance our relationship at the speed of light. Most people use the second date to get to know each other and engage in shared interests. Not for Rebecca. The second date was her opportunity to ask me if I wanted a wedding in Fiji or if I'd prefer a traditional church-photos-reception ceremony.

After years in the dating world, you'd think I'd have learned enough to know when to pull the plug. Unfortunately for me, either my skull was too thick or

my heart was too soft. I continued to see Rebecca despite the red flags. Things went downhill fast.

On the third date, she said, "I love you." On the fourth, she told me her parents were coming into town and she wanted me to meet them. On our fifth and final date, she announced she was selling her house and asked when she could start moving her things into my place. I told her we should date other people and got the hell out of there.

The problem was that she never stopped calling.

I sat and gave my coffee-drinking-task a second try now that I was safely seated at my desk without any shocking voicemails. When I put the mug to my lips and tilted, only a little coffee remained. I drained the cup in one quick swallow. The day was not starting well.

Too distracted to focus on the deposition, I trudged from my office to the first-floor cafeteria. Most people stocked up on their morning energy boosts when they arrived at work, so I wasn't surprised to see just a handful of employees. Among them, one face stood out.

"Aren't you supposed to be one floor up taking Harrison's calls?" I joked by way of greeting.

She turned. Crisa Brant was one of the executive secretaries employed by the firm's founder, but she was the only one who possessed intelligence to rival her stunning looks.

"It's Danish Day." She held up a pastry with a smile. "I always let the first fifteen minutes of calls go to voicemail on Danish Day."

Crisa was close to my age, perhaps a year or two older, and had a smile that could brighten the darkest mood. She started working at Harrison & Crowe sixteen months ago, and we'd met after she took the last corned beef sandwich. I offered to buy it from her for twenty bucks. She laughingly declined and told me the last corned beef was priceless.

Since then, we chatted every time we encountered each other in the cafeteria. Something about her always put a bounce in my step.

"Danish Day isn't as good as Cookie Day," I teased.

"Are you kidding?" She cried in mock indignation. "Cookie Day is great, but Danish Day is the real thriller. Danishes are special. They're an *art*. You have to respect Danish Day."

I laughed, her wit and energy lifting the dark cloud of Rebecca's voicemail. My day was suddenly looking better.

Chapter Three

Crisa

Slade Doyle was one of those men who had the world at his feet. He was forty-nine, devastatingly handsome, impressively smart, and wealthy to boot. I'd be kidding myself if I pretended I didn't notice his assets, but our conversations were casual and light-hearted. Besides, I didn't consider him a dateable option. Slade might as well have been living on a different planet given the lack of similarities between us, and he was relegated to the part of my brain that dreamt up romantic fantasies I knew would never come true.

"How have you been?" I mentally patted myself on the back for not stumbling over my words, doing my best to look happy to see him without being over the top.

"I've been so wrapped up in this deposition I'm working on that I wasn't able to make it down for corned beef day," he said, making a face. His voice was low, something underneath the light humor hinting at a level of education and culture that most men could only dream of. The tone was irresistibly sexy.

I raised my eyebrows and scoffed, pretending to be offended on his behalf. "The injustice of it all! Who cares about prosecuting criminals when corned beef is on the line?"

His face morphed into a full-blown smile, the laugh lines in his face deepening and accenting his rugged features. He shook his head playfully. "The sacrifices we make. But what about you? Anything new and exciting since I saw you last?"

My mind went to Lawrence Nader and our unfulfilling tryst, but I wasn't about to tell Slade something so personal.

"Pretty good," I shrugged. "I signed up for yoga."

"Yeah?" His eyebrows lifted toward his hairline, which was beginning to streak with silver. "How was that?"

"I wanted to kick the instructor."

He chuckled, a purring sound that sent little prickles of delight up my arms. I loved the fact that I could make him laugh without trying.

"And why would you want to kick a perfectly nice yoga instructor?"

I sighed, gesturing vaguely. "She's one of those twenty-somethings with a body like a gymnast and a voice like a cartoon character. I'm on my mat trying to figure out how to get my leg behind my head while she tells me I need to *release my demons*. She reminds me of my daughter."

He leaned against a table with his arms crossed and a broad grin on his attractive face. "And how are the kids?"

"They're good. Lisa had her baby, so I get calls at all hours of the night asking if hiccups are dangerous or what to do with leftover milk. Terry started his oldest in T-ball yesterday, and David's still insisting marriage is just another way for the government to keep tabs on us."

Slade smiled. "He sounds like a big thinker."

"He's the baby. He wants to make sure he's not his brother's clone," I explained, rolling my eyes.

"Well, if it makes you feel any better, I'm not the eldest in my family but I ended up being a lawyer." He motioned to himself as if to prove that children who weren't the eldest could succeed in traditional careers.

"There's a world of difference between 'not the eldest' and 'baby of the family.' In any case, the day

David becomes a lawyer will be the day I would like yoga." A tiny smirk played at the corners of my lips.

Slade chuckled again, and I couldn't stop myself from smiling back. Aside from the credentials that established him as a good catch, he was easy to talk to, and I relished that quality. Our conversations were tension-free, with no uncomfortable silence. I could tell him the tiny details of my life with no awkwardness or shame, and he always displayed genuine interest. It was like we were friends, though we never spent time together outside of the firm's cafeteria.

He straightened his shoulders. "So, what are your plans for tonight?"

"I have a date with the newest Dan Brown book," I mumbled, sinking my teeth into the light dough of my pastry. Its sweet, fruity center was exquisite.

"Maybe you'd like to go on a date with me instead."

I stared at him, my jaw freezing mid-chew as I processed his words. I thought I'd tricked myself into hearing something he didn't say, or that my disappointing Lawrence Nader experience had me desperate for a pleasant time with an intriguing man.

I had decided to stop dating? My past attempts had a range of outcomes, the best of which were yawn-inducing letdowns. Dating was a waste of time that I could invest into something more meaningful like deepening platonic friendships or finding a hobby to pursue. At least, that was what I kept trying to tell myself.

"I—what?" I winced at my graceful response.

"Would you like to have dinner with me tonight?" Slade was cool, calm, and collected, despite a possible rejection, while I drooled cherry filling. Typical.

I swallowed my bite half-chewed, choking me on the way down. I cleared my throat to cover a gag. "I don't think we can do that. Isn't dating a co-worker against company policy?"

"If I were your boss, yes. But you're Harrison's subordinate, not mine. Plus, our jobs never require us to work together. Technically, we're just two people who collect our checks from the same place," he explained. Holding up his hands, he added, "If you don't want to or feel uncomfortable, no hard feelings."

"No!" I yelped. *Smooth, Crisa. Was that a new soprano note?* Reining myself in, I repeated, "No, as long as it won't cost either of us our jobs, I could have dinner with you." *What the heck am I doing?* My brain and my mouth weren't working in tandem. I let out a small sigh and wiped my mouth with a napkin.

His eyes sparkled, the cafeteria lighting reflecting the grays and blues into a mesmerizing whirlpool. "Great. Do you need to go home first, or should I swing by your desk at the end of the day?"

"Come by my desk. It'll give me an excuse to leave on time for once," I told him.

"Perfect." He smoothed his tie and smiled. "I'd better get my coffee and head back up. My morning didn't exactly start on the right foot."

"I see," I commented, gesturing to the drying stains on his shirt.

He smirked, gave me a little wave, and departed for one of the automatic coffee machines. I glanced at the clock over the door and promptly sped towards the elevators. My usual fifteen-minute break for Danish Day had turned into nearly half an hour, and Mr. Harrison would not be thrilled if his voicemail was full to bursting.

As I stood in the elevator, I realized the heat of my fingers caused the Danish to become soft and sticky while I'd talked with Slade. I wrapped the Danish haphazardly in a napkin so I could toss it once I got to my desk. I wasn't really hungry anymore.

My belly twisted, rolling with excitement and nerves. I couldn't wait for five o'clock. Every second suddenly seemed to last an hour. Would this date wind up a massive mistake like the others? Or would it break my losing streak with men? Either way, I forced myself to repeat a single mantra: *And no sex on the first date!*

At least I was certain of one thing: Danish Day was *definitely* my favorite day.

Chapter Four

Slade

I had no intention of asking Crisa for a date when I went down to the cafeteria, but she was such a breath of fresh air that I couldn't help myself. Still reeling from Rebecca's unexpected voicemail, finding myself face to face with a woman like Crisa who was grounded, funny, and smart- I couldn't *not* ask her.

I'd considered asking her several times before, but with her husband's death still recent I didn't want to infringe on her grieving. I cringed internally as the words jumped from my lips unbidden, half wishing I could take them back. Apparently, luck was on my side, though, because she said yes!

My office felt friendlier when I returned. The wad of wet Post-It notes were still piled on my desk, and the coffee stain had settled into the carpet, but I didn't

care. *Let the cleaning crew work their magic.* Humming, I pulled my emergency white dress shirt from my office closet and changed.

I wanted five o'clock to come quickly, but time would drag if I didn't occupy myself. With my back to the wall clock, I sat and threw my concentration into the thick deposition file staring at me.

The tactic worked. I zoomed through the morning, skipped lunch, took calls, made a few appointments for Monday, and responded to some long overdue emails. When I finally checked the time, it was a quarter to five.

I meandered to the second floor, hoping to kill the remaining time. Crisa sat at her desk, and it thrilled me to see the flash of excitement cross her face when our eyes locked.

"Are you ready?" I asked.

"Technically, I'm supposed to work another six minutes." She glanced at the tiny clock in the corner of her desk. "But, yes, I'm ready."

We exited the building. She chattered all the way to my car about Harrison and his tendency to micromanage. I nodded sympathetically, remembering my own experiences with him.

When I started at the firm as a fresh-off-the-grad-stage lawyer over two decades ago, Harrison attached himself to my hip for a year to make sure I handled clients and cases the way he would. Thankfully, our paths didn't find much reason to cross these days. He wasn't a bad guy, and he was an excellent lawyer, but he was one of those types of people I couldn't handle in doses larger than a baby spoon.

"Don't worry too much about it," I advised, opening the passenger door of my car for her. "He'll slowly back off so much you'll think he disappeared."

"Oh, no, I don't mind! This firm is his baby. He's allowed to have high standards," she said.

She amazed me with her open-mindedness. I stood dumbfounded for several seconds, only remembering that I needed to close the car door when she shot me a curious look. What I had assumed was a complaint was truly just Crisa making an honest observation. This woman was refreshing beyond belief.

The restaurant I'd chosen was a small Italian eatery with six tables and a hefty price tag. It wasn't lavish, but it was intimate and authentic, one of those unforgettable evening experiences. Crisa eyed the interior with interest as the host led us to a table.

"Have you been here?" I asked over the gentle music.

"No," she sounded delighted. "But I kind of wish I had. It smells heavenly."

"Just wait. The food is extraordinary. The owner is from Firenze and does all the cooking himself."

We didn't say much as we pored over the menu. When the waiter delivered our drinks and took our orders, our eyes met.

"So," she began. "I know we talk a lot in the cafeteria, but I don't know much about you."

"What would you like to know?" I asked, leaning back in my chair comfortably.

"Name, rank, and serial number," she joked.

I chuckled. "I'm not complicated. No kids, never married. This is the twenty-third year I've been with the firm. I hate golf, which is not looked upon kindly in lawyer circles, but I love to rock-climb when I get the chance."

"On a rock wall?"

"Only if there are no real rocks around."

"Very nice," she said with an approving nod. "Continue."

I paused. It was difficult to pick my most interesting details on a whim, and what I found interesting might bore her. "I used to have a dog named Hulk."

"As a kid?"

"No, just a couple years ago," I clarified.

She giggled. "Manly. No cats?"

"Allergic."

"How about a hamster?"

Crisa was sharp. There weren't many people who I could go back and forth with like this, and the speed of our banter was exhilarating. "My sister had one when I was four, but it escaped and we never found it."

"You have a sister?" She asked, crooking a brow.

"Yeah," I nodded. "One older sister and one younger brother. I'm the middle child."

"Uh oh," she remarked.

I raised a brow. "Uh oh? Is that bad?"

"Oh, definitely." A small grin illuminated her face, and I could tell she was teasing me. Her confidence was arousing. "Middle children come with a host of problems, you know. Constantly needing attention, since they didn't get it growing up. Very judgmental because they're usually the most successful. Things like that."

"Interesting. And what are you?" I grinned.

"The youngest!" She announced. "That's a completely different kind of trouble."

I laughed. "I would imagine. You said it yourself that there's something unique about the baby of the family." I punctuated my words with a wink and internally cheered when I caught the slight blush on her cheeks in response.

I had never encountered a woman quite like Crisa, and the chemistry between us was the kind of

electricity I'd only heard about in bad rom-coms. However, something deeper lay beneath the superficial attraction. She fascinated me and I wanted to know everything about her. The need to nurture my connection with her was strong, as was my rising physical desire.

Nothing about her was unattractive. Soft, walnut-colored hair hung in loose curls around her shoulders and framed her delicate, heart-shaped face. She had a womanly figure, which I appreciated far more than the skinny, leggy forms of twenty-year-old girls. A ring of amber encircled rich brown eyes, and they drew me in as we spoke. Her beauty melted me. We'd developed a casual friendship in the last six months at Harrison & Crowe, and I knew she was far more than a pretty face. She was beautiful, to be sure, but my interest in her was rooted in every facet of who she was- not just the visible ones. Crisa's kindness, intelligence, and warmth made her the amazing woman I had the pleasure of dining with tonight. Those stunning looks of hers were a bonus.

As the server returned with our food, a realization struck me. I wanted to pursue something meaningful with Crisa, and I hoped with all my heart we could.

Chapter Five

Crisa

My date with Slade was amazing, probably because it didn't seem like a date at all. We laughed and joked through dinner, asked each other questions, and conversed like two good friends. It wasn't until he drove me back to the firm for my car that the mood shifted, and what a shift! The air in the car was thick with tension as we pulled into the parking lot, and I found myself unsure of how to proceed. *Did I really want us to go our separate ways?* I wasn't sure what pace I wanted with Slade.

"Thank you for keeping me company," he said, and his eyes met mine.

He opened my door and helped me out, and we stood beside my vehicle. I held my purse open, ready to fish my keys out.

"Of course!" I replied. My nerves were rattled leading up to the date, but they had vanished once I sat down with Slade at the restaurant. It was strange- I barely knew him, but I felt more relaxed with him than I had in the last decade. Was it the backbone of our casual friendship that helped create that vibe, or was it the man himself? "Thank you for the invite. I had a wonderful time and the food was to die for."

"It was my pleasure."

My stomach churned as my mind briefly flashed to Lawrence Nader saying those exact words. The memory of the cooling sheets on my skin and the tone of Lawrence's voice was so vivid, but I blinked hard. *Slade isn't him.* I shook my head to erase the image.

His voice dropped, probing, and his gaze warmed as he stared at me. Our bodies were closer than they would have been during a conversation in the cafeteria. The logical part of my brain knew that if I wanted something deeper than sex, I needed to step back. As I caught a whiff of his cologne, however, the logical part of my brain quickly took a back seat to my searing desire for him. I noticed that our mouths were inches apart, separated only by scant centimeters and propriety.

"Well," I said softly, "I guess I'll see you on Monday."

I gazed at him through my lashes, my heart beating in my throat, waiting to see what he would do. He caressed my chin with a gentle finger.

"I don't know if I want to wait that long," he murmured.

My pulse quickened, and before I could move or speak, his lips were on mine.

The kiss took me by surprise. Hot and needy, our mouths melded together. One of his hands slid to the small of my back and pulled me closer until our forms were flush against each other. The tip of his tongue traced my lower lip as he darted experimentally past my teeth, and I received the intimate gesture by massaging his tongue with mine. My entire body came alive beneath the heat in his kiss, every nerve prickling and dancing with anticipation. I knew I liked Slade as soon as I met him in the cafeteria, but this was a different level of compatibility. This was sensual and erotic and everything I had dreamed of growing up.

When we broke apart, I forced myself to resist inviting him home. My foray into the world of casual sex was something I wanted to keep separate from Slade. He wasn't a theory I was testing, and he was no Lawrence Nader.

"Are you free tomorrow afternoon?" His voice tinged with hope.

I smiled teasingly. "Not to go rock-climbing."

"How about some time on Liberty Lake?" He brushed a strand of hair from my forehead. "I have a new boat, and I was thinking of taking it out."

I wasn't surprised that he had a boat. He was a wealthy, single lawyer, after all. Nevertheless, I found myself giddy.

"That sounds great," I agreed.

He bent down to kiss me again, this time with gentle affection rather than passion.

"I'll call you," he promised. "But first, I need your number."

We exchanged numbers, then as he got into his car, I swooned a little as he waited until I was in my car making sure I left the parking lot safely. It was such a small gesture, but it spoke worlds about his sense of chivalry- something I found to be sorely lacking in all of the men I had dated previously.

As I drove home, I didn't bother turning on the radio. My heart raced almost as fast as my mind, and I tried to process the unexpected turn my weekend was taking. The palpable chemistry Slade and I had turned my brain into a useless puddle. Our date lacked the tense awkwardness I typically expected from first dates, and we shared a genuine interest in one another that came effortlessly. He excited me in a way I hadn't known since I met Alan, in fact, I couldn't remember if Alan had ever excited me this way even at the very beginning.

It was the horrible truth. Slade was intriguing, handsome, sweet, and he had a way of looking at me like I was the only woman in the room who mattered. Perhaps it was Alan's admission of his affairs and the lingering effect they'd made on me, but Slade's presence and company had a precious value that none of his money or material things could match. He made me feel beautiful, sensual, and wanted.

As I turned onto my street, my mind drifted to our date the next day. We'd be on a boat in the middle of gorgeous Liberty Lake together, isolated from the rest of the world all day. That could lead to any number of things, including hot, steamy, sweaty sex I had barely resisted indulging in at the end of our date.

Should I rush it? A part of my brain longed for the slow courtship of old romance, no matter how cheesy it might be. In any case, tomorrow's events would certainly be a test of my resolve in the face of temptation.

By the time I placed my keys on the hook by the door, I decided I wasn't ready to test the fragile new relationship I was hoping to build with Slade. I waited an hour, then called him. He didn't answer, so I left him a voicemail.

"Hey, it's Crisa. Uh. Er. I'm so sorry, but I have to, I paused to find the right word, *take a rain-check on our date tomorrow.* Excuses rolled through my mind, *my son is coming into town on business, and I agreed to have lunch with him.* And so I wouldn't scare him off, I added, *I'll make it up to you by buying you lunch one day at work next week, if you're free. I'm really sorry!"*

I felt guilty for lying before I even hung up the phone. I called my son and made lunch plans for the next day so at least it wasn't a total lie. Deep down, I knew Slade would understand even though he had no kids of his own. He knew how important my kids were to me, and I knew he'd never ask me to put time with him before them.

My lie meant I'd bought myself time to decide what I wanted to do about Slade, but as I got ready for bed and crawled under the covers, I realized I already knew the answer. I wanted him, I was just terrified of all the ways that things could go wrong. Hopefully at some point I'd be able to make it up to him, but for now, I just had to keep my fingers crossed that he wouldn't hold this against me.

Chapter Six

Slade

When I heard Crisa's voicemail, I couldn't help smiling. Her apology sounded sweet and innocent, like she almost believed I'd be angry for postponing the date. Of course, my lawyer training has given my insight to identify verbal signs of lying; using small words, stumbling before speaking and so on. I knew she probably didn't have plans. with her son, or that, if she did, they were made after she left her message. Her words were rushed, and her voice was breathless, as if she was hurriedly reading a script.

I understood her hesitation; our personalities sparked when we were together. There was a sort of magic between us which gave me similar reservations about progressing our relationship too quickly. Was

this real? Marriage had never been an option for me. I just never found a woman who made me want to spend the rest of my days with her. Frankly, it was frightening and exciting. But that hadn't stopped me from exploring relationships to see how far things could go. I believed in giving love a chance, no matter how unlikely it seemed, hence, my Rebecca situation. I shuddered at the thought of her name.

I took a quick shower so I could take a few minutes to think about what I wanted to say when I returned her call. The water running over my face was calming. After which I toweled off before going to my bedside table and grabbing my phone. Her voicemail picked up, and I chuckled.

"Ah, I love a nice game of phone tag, especially when my date postpones our plans. Seriously though, lunch next week sounds great. I know how much you love your kiddos, and time with them is important. So, no worries. Although I have to warn you, it won't come cheap, since it was you who canceled. I grinned like a schoolboy, *just let me know which day you're free, and we'll get together then. Bye, darlin'."* Darlin', did I just say that? It might have been wrong to use such a personal name, hopefully she'll realize it's because I like her.

I didn't hear from Crisa all weekend, but when I got to the office on Monday the oversized calendar on my desk had "Lunch with Crisa at 12" scrawled in bright red letters across Monday's date block. If any other woman had been so bold as to assume I'd just pencil in time like that, I'd have ended the relationship right then, but Crisa's lovely script letters made me smile, as I remembered our date. I called and reserved a table at a nearby brunch place.

We met in front of the building at noon. I nodded my head in the direction of the restaurant. Conversation flowed effortlessly as we walked, and it continued while we waited for our food to arrive. She caught me up on her visit with her son, and I recapped my uneventful weekend at home.

I didn't press her on rescheduling our boating date, much as I wanted to. If she needed time to take things slow and decide what she wanted, I could give her that. Each time I saw or thought of Crisa my heart gave an extra beat. I didn't want to risk ruining things before they'd begun. If we could keep seeing each other on a regular basis, I didn't need boat dates to be happy. Lunch ended too fast, but we parted with a promise to see each other again soon.

As it turned out, the next few weeks were crazy. I had dinner meetings with new potential clients, weekend paperwork became routine, and I rarely got to see Crisa outside of work. However, we had lunch almost every day. I started walking her to her car in

the evenings, even when I had to stay late, just to spend a few extra minutes with her. Those stolen moments were the bright spot of my entire day. I learned a great deal about Crisa, and the more time I spent with her, the more time I wanted to have. I hoped she felt the same way.

Two months went by before I brought up our lake date again. Once I found an opportunity, I jumped on in. Crisa and I were having dinner on a Friday evening, and when our conversation turned to our weekend plans, I asked her to join me for a date on the boat. She gladly accepted. I didn't sense any hesitation on her part this time. A runabout of butterflies sailed in my stomach at the knowledge that I would spend a whole day with her.

The sun glared, relentlessly beating down from above with searing rays and blinding light. I squinted into the rays, enjoying the way they reflected off the surface of the water. We were in the middle of the lake, and the breeze was a cool balance to the heat of the sun. Content, I glanced at Crisa as I turned off the boat.

Gorgeous. I'd only seen her outside of work attire twice, and even then, her outfits had bordered on Sunday best. She always wore her pencil skirts and button-down blouses beautifully, but I had to choke back the hiss of air that escaped my lungs at the sight of her lounging on the boat. Her light brown hair tumbled over her shoulder in a loose ponytail that grazed the nape of her slender neck. Her pulled back hair revealed the full silhouette of her delicate face, over which she'd propped a pair of glamorous, oversized sunglasses. The swimsuit she wore was one of those complicated cutout one-pieces that reminded me of a geometry figure, but it hugged the curves of her body while still leaving enough to the imagination. My eyes drifted to her legs, which she stretched across one of the bench seats. I noticed her painted toenails, a deep plum color that offset her lavender swimsuit. Gazing at her, I had trouble believing she was fifty-one.

"So, now what?" She called over the lake breeze, a grin edging across her face.

I bent over, while still in the captain's chair to the cooler and extracted two bottles. "Beer?" I offered.

Crisa nodded, and I got to my feet and handed it to her. I tossed the cap into the plastic bag I'd tied to the back of a chair for trash. She took a long drink and settled back in the seat and stared up at the clear, turquoise sky through her lenses.

"I could stay out here forever," she mused.

"Me too," I agreed, sitting next to her on the bench seat. Crisa took the cue, slipping her legs off the bench to make room. I wanted her closer to me

without moving in too close, so I settled for sitting with my thigh against hers. *Boundaries.*

"I've always loved being out on the water. I don't know why it took me so long to get a boat."

"Did you live on the lake as a kid?" She asked as she dropped her head to look at me.

I shook my head.

"Nope, I lived in a suburban split-level next door to a woman who had more parakeets than visitors." Crisa laughed, prompting a smile from me as I continued. "My dad was a big fisherman. I used to go out with him a lot, and every family vacation had to be somewhere he could fish from sunup to sundown."

"Oh my God, I haven't fished in *years*," Crisa exclaimed. "The last time I did, my kids were little. Terry hooked Lisa in the leg, and we had to take her to the emergency room because the thing was embedded so deep."

I chuckled and rose from my seat. Curious, she opened her mouth to speak, but I wagged a finger to silence her and trekked to the rear of the boat. Opening the bench seat, I retrieved two fishing rods and turned to face her with a questioning smirk.

"Interested?" I asked, wriggling my brows.

Crisa laughed, spinning herself off of the cushioned bench to come closer to me. "I can't believe you brought those!" She cried. "Did you plan on fishing?"

"No, I stuck them in the boat after I brought it home," I explained, leaning them against the freestanding passenger chair and bending down again to retrieve the tackle box. "I don't have live bait, but I've got lures we could try. I doubt the fish are biting since it's the middle of the day, but, hey, what do you say?"

"I say, if there's a fish to be caught, I'll catch it!" She declared.

Closing the bench seat, I glanced over my shoulder. "I don't know. Of the two of us, only one spent nearly every weekend of his childhood on a boat with a rod in his hand."

Her lips twitched, barely holding back a giggle.

"That sounds perverted. I hope your dad wasn't nearby," she said.

I handed her one of the fishing poles, trying to hide my smile at her teasing.

"Don't hook me," I warned.

She grinned. My heart leapt, and it dawned on me that she already had.

Chapter Seven

Crisa

I stared down at the lake, trying to spot any sign of fish in its depths. The mud had long settled, but the water was dark enough that I couldn't make out much of anything. Slade's voice interrupted my trance.

"What are you looking for?" He kidded.

"Just looking and thinking." I leaned back from the edge and closed my eyes. "It's peaceful." He'd picked a lovely spot for fishing, and I relished the atmosphere.

A breeze drifted through the air, and my mind went with it. After all the men in my life, the one-night stands, the lifetime of regrets- none of it had prepared me for Slade. I couldn't help but wonder if he was too good to be true or would he end up as

another miserable memory. It just didn't make sense that an attractive man like Slade who had so much to offer wouldn't have a special lady in his life.

Determined to solve the mystery since I'd been seeing him for a few months now, I opened my eyes and turned to him.

"So, what's your fatal flaw?" It was blunt and harsher than I intended, but Slade took it with good humor.

"That's a fair question. It's natural to be a little skeptical."

"Not skeptical," I corrected. "Just wondering how a guy like you is single."

He stroked his chin and pretended to meditate. I loved the way he warmed my heart and made my stomach flutter. He cocked his head, and for one terrible second, I feared he'd read my thoughts.

His face brightened. "The huge coffee stain on my shirt a couple of months ago wasn't enough evidence of a flaw?"

"It told me you might either be clumsy or messy, but those are hardly fatal flaws," I said. "Is it possible you don't have one?"

"Oh, I wouldn't say that," he said. With a serious expression, he leaned toward me and took a breath. "I guess I never met the right woman."

I bit my lip. Something in him both calmed and excited me. A wave of vulnerability washed over me, and I hoped I hadn't made another embarrassing mistake by asking him so directly.

It took a few seconds for me to notice Slade staring. I met his gaze, he blinked then backed up a few inches. His cheeks flushed a subtle pink, and I smirked.

"What are you thinking?" He asked, regaining his cool demeanor. He leaned against the side of the boat, fishing pole in one hand.

Feeling brave, I tossed my hair off my shoulder. "Being with you frightens me, but it makes me feel good, too."

"Hmm, I think I know what you mean." He jerked his fishing line upward, then let it settle back into place.

My heart skipped. It had been a long time since I felt anything like this for a man. I was rusty with guys whose chemistry kept my blood humming. After Alan and his affairs, I no longer believed such a rapport was possible. I stared at Slade's strong manicured hand as it rested on the reel.

I wasn't sure what I wanted, but I could either become half of the solution or half of the problem. I was simultaneously thrilled and terrified, unsure if I

could trust my emotions. Was this my desperation and grief, or could this be real?

A tug on the line pulled me from my thoughts. I shook myself from la-la-land and gripped the pole. Slade moved toward me with wide eyes.

"Something on the line?"

"Yep," I nodded.

He moved closer. "Stay calm and keep your grip firm."

He placed his hand on mine, his chest pressed against my back. With a gentle, deep voice, he helped me guide the pole. *Can he feel the thunderous hammering of my heart?*

He steadied my grip and I started reeling in the fish. A harder pull on the line jerked me from his hands.

"Oh my god, what sort of fish is this?" I yanked the pole, trying to regain control. Slade stayed close, but gave me space.

The fish tugged again, and adrenaline roared through me, my heart racing. I gave the pole one last flick before abruptly finding myself ass-first on the boat floor.

He laughed and offered his hand to help me hoist myself off the ground. When I recovered from my daze, I began giggling before devolving into full-fledged laughter with him. He took the pole and pulled the now-empty line from the water. The fish managed to escape with its life, but it took some of my pride with it.

He raised an eyebrow as he put down the fishing pole. "It was a good attempt." He smiled, and I found myself enthralled with how sweet he was. "Want to try again?"

I grimaced and shook my head.

"Not just yet." I pushed a strand of hair from my eyes and shifted my weight.

Slade laughed again. "Hey, don't take it personal. The fish fled because it didn't want to be fileted."

I put my fists on my hips and cocked my head.

"Is that your special one-liner? How long have you been waiting to use that one, sir?" I tossed my hair off my shoulder again.

He paused, thoughtful. "I'd be lying if I said I wasn't trying to impress you." His face fell. I focused on the sudden change of emotion and my heart froze. He took a deep breath and continued. "But I think I'm trying harder with you than I ever have before."

"I won't judge," I assured him. "I know I'm not the first woman to enter your life." I brushed my bangs back from my face and watched him, waiting to see what he would say or do next.

Slade stepped into my space and drew me closer; his body heat was a welcome contrast to the cool

breeze from the lake. The boat rocked, and I took a seat on the bench. He took my face in his large, gentle hands and leaned down to press his mouth to mine. Kissing Slade was as intoxicating as a rich wine. Another soft breeze caressed my skin and I shivered.

He pressed closer, kissing the corner of my mouth. His warm breath brushed my lips, and the soft pressure of his body against mine made me weak.

I forced myself to break away from his addictive kiss.

"Hold on," I gasped.

"Of course." Slade jumped back, and slid himself to the side.

"It's just— I really like you, and I don't— I— our dates are always incredible, and I enjoy spending time with you. I just don't want to mess things up by rushing into anything."

A calm, understanding smile dispelled my awkwardness in an instant. He leaned in to give me a warm peck on the lips and rose from the bench.

He stared across the lake, shielding his eyes from the sun with his hand. Then, he reached for the cooler and grabbed two more beers, a bowl of pasta salad, and a container of cold roasted chicken.

"Are you hungry?"

Grateful that he seemed to be on the same page as me about our relationship, I shot him a warm smile. "Ravenous!"

Chapter 8

Slade

I pulled up on a small handle embedded in the deck, then lifted as a small floor piece telescoped upward locking into place. I then reached into the bench seat and schlepped out a tri-folded table top. Once it was secured into place, I prepared plates for us and then sat across from Crisa. The brief silence while we ate gave me time to study her. Our close encounter moments before had brought a light pink flush to her cheeks, and I lowered my gaze so she wouldn't notice me staring.

Her blunt words were a surprise. She was forthright, and didn't hesitate to ask why I wasn't married. Such candor was a new experience for me, and I liked it. Women usually made assumptions and

tried to wrap me around their fingers rather than ask a simple question.

The abrupt change of events flustered me. I wanted things to go further, but did she feel the same? I thought so, but if I moved too fast, there might not be another date. I froze mid-bite at the thought of not being able to see Crisa again.

She must have noticed, because she put down her fork.

"Don't tell me there's a fishing lure in the salad," she said. Her light tone contrasted with her wrinkled brow. I shook my head.

"There's something I need to tell you."

Her eyes widened. I had one chance to say what was on my mind without mucking it up, so I moved closer to her.

"I'm sorry if I was pushy." She opened her mouth to speak, but I stopped her. "The last thing I want is to frighten you. No good ever comes from casting off too fast."

The tension melted from her face, and she smiled.

"Exactly! Why rush, when we have plenty of time to screw things up?" She giggled. I released the breath I was holding.

"When the time is right, we can screw up, down, sideways, or on our heads, if you want," she continued coyly, biting her lip. Her face was innocent and seductive, and I wanted nothing more than to contradict my speech and pin her to the ground. Instead, I reached for my plate and busied myself with a piece of chicken.

A muffled jazz ringtone chimed. Crisa scanned the boat until she spotted her purse. She scooted over to grab her cell phone. Her lips moved as she skimmed the screen. Then, she started laughing.

I frowned, puzzled. My inquisitive expression made her laugh harder. When she could breathe, she held up the phone.

"My daughter," she snorted, then took a deep breath. "My daughter, the one with the new baby. She's texting wanting to know if carrots could change a baby's skin color!" She succumbed to another fit of giggles. I didn't understand the joke, but her musical laugh made me chuckle along with her.

She centered herself and wiped her eyes.

"I'm trying to find a way to explain carotenemia without giving her a heart attack." I realized what she was talking about and my chuckles deepened into a belly laugh. Carotenemia was something that happened to babies when they ate a bunch of orange or yellow fruits and vegetables. My sister had it as an infant, and her skin was a vibrant shade of yellow. I imagined Crisa's daughter believing the baby food

had some magic skin dying chemical, and I had to resist the urge to guffaw.

Crisa sighed. "I guess I better help the poor girl with her stress. You don't mind if I cut things a little short, do you?"

I shook my head. "Family always comes first. I have a huge stack of paperwork to finish before Monday morning anyway."

She folded her hands against her chest. "Thank you. You're an angel!"

"With a devilish fatal flaw." I waggled my eyebrows.

"I know a great exorcist," she said, eyes sparkling. Was it my imagination, or was she getting prettier each time I looked at her?

While she gathered her things, I steered the boat to the dock. The water was smooth, and we made great time. I killed the boat's engine and took Crisa's hand. We walked in silence until we reached her car.

I stepped back so she could unlock her door.

"Don't give your poor daughter too much hell," I teased.

"I'll be a good girl, Mr. Doyle," she said while tossing her tote onto the passenger seat.

"I hope not. I'll call you tomorrow to see how everything went."

She nodded as she slid into the seat. "I look forward to it."

I watched her leave the lot. As I made my way home, I made a mental list of places she might like on our next date.

The next morning, I dove into my paperwork first thing and lost track of time. At 11:30pm, I woke up face down on the last two documents. When I noticed the time, I was furious with myself for disappointing Crisa. What would she be thinking? I hoped she wouldn't think I was retaliating for the time she canceled on me. The thought formed a boulder in my stomach. Somehow, I had to make it up to her.

At 3 a.m., still furious with myself, I decided to send her a text, hoping her phone wasn't near. I'd hate to wake her. I finally fell into a fitful sleep. When my work alarm rang, I grabbed my phone and leaped out of bed. I had no idea if any florist would be open this early, but I was desperate to make amends.

An elderly sounding woman answered on the third ring. I didn't give her time to launch into her rehearsed greeting.

"Hi. My name is Slade Doyle. I need to know how soon you can have two dozen of your best pink roses delivered to the office." I paused. She said they could be there in an hour. I placed my order.

"The name of the recipient is Crisa Brant. Yes, here's the address." I gave her all the details and rushed to finish dressing.

That was the first step of Operation: Earn Crisa's Forgiveness.

Chapter 9

Crisa

I crawled into bed at midnight, embarrassed that I had carried the phone around with me all night. Of course, he hadn't call. This was too good to be true, and I should have known better. I'd made a rash assumption and now I was paying the price. I sniffled and tried to keep the tears from falling as I reminded myself that he was a long-time bachelor. It was foolish of me to believe we had a deeper connection. After wallowing sleeplessly until 5 a.m., I jerked myself from bed and got ready for work.

As I drove, I decided to avoid Slade. I stopped near the office for coffee so I wouldn't see him in the cafeteria. By the firm's clock, I was 30 minutes early.

The back stairs seemed a better option over the elevators. No sense in taking chances.

By the time I reached my desk, I was sweating. With a sigh, I collapsed in my chair and my elbow brushed up against a giant bouquet of flowers. *Great, some delivery dink made a mistake.* I rolled my eyes; my desk wasn't a drop-off table. The card would tell me who the lucky girl was.

I searched for the card, slowly turning the vase and admiring the exquisite pink roses. The little envelope was printed with the florist's name and below was my name!

Sweet Crisa was printed on the card within the envelope, and behind that was a folded piece of paper. I unfurled the note.

You can't imagine how sorry I am for not calling. I passed out face-first in a stack of papers. If the sight of my face isn't too repulsive, I'd love to have lunch with you today. Meet me in the lobby at 11:45. I hope you come. P.S. I hope my text didn't wake you.

Hopefully Yours,

Slade

What text? I fumbled through my purse and snatched out my phone. Sure enough, there was a text time-stamped at 3:01 a.m. I laughed through tears. That was the sweetest thing any man had ever done for me, and I was foolish to think Slade would dismiss me and run. It hadn't been fair to project all of my past negative experiences onto him when he had been nothing but thoughtful and respectful to me. I pictured him asleep and drooling over affidavits. If it was that rough of a day, the least I could do was meet him for lunch.

The morning dragged. On most days, finding five minutes of peace was a chore, but for some reason I only answered three calls, five emails, and one fax. It struck me as odd, but I couldn't think much while my mind did jumping-jacks in anticipation of seeing Slade.

At 11:30 I freshened up and headed to the lobby. My heart threatened to break through my ribs, but I tried to look casual. Mr. Harrison was talking to the head receptionist. I hoped it wouldn't occur to him that I should be at my desk. When he waved me over, I was certain he had.

I gave him a weak smile.

"Hello, Mr. Harrison," I said. He didn't appear upset.

"Good morning, Ms. Brant! Heading out for your lunch date?" He smiled. I nodded, relieved.

"Have a wonderful time!" he said, and then headed for the elevators.

Wait— What—? How did he know I had a lunch date? I shook my head. No one else did, so how could he. He was either assuming or it was a lucky guess.

I saw Slade leaning on a block glass wall near the front door. Somehow, he was more handsome than he had been on Saturday. Maybe it was because his roses and note showed me how beautiful his heart was. He had me hooked.

He must have noticed my reflection in the glass because he turned to greet me. Without a word, he wrapped his arms around me and squeezed until I couldn't breathe. At last, he broke the silence.

"I wasn't sure you'd come," he whispered. I pried myself from his embrace, then looked up at him.

"I had to see if you were wearing your legal document sleeping mask." I smiled. He laughed, and led me to the door.

"Not today, but later I can show you the appeals pajamas I'm working on," he said, and I giggled.

"Sounds sexy." I pulled my purse strap further up on my shoulder. "So, where are we going?"

He pulled a silk cloth from his pocket. "Do you trust me?"

I nodded, surprised, then turned.

Slade placed it over my eyes and tied it in place, then took my arm.

"Let me guide you, darling." He led me to his car. Soft jazz music played when the car started. I had no idea what he had in mind, but my body was tingling, every nerve ending on fire.

"If you wanted to kidnap me, sir, all you had to do was ask." I tried to look seductive, but it was difficult with half my face covered by the blindfold.

"It's funny you should say that—" his voice trailed off.

I guessed my asking him why would ruin whatever he had planned, so I settled into the seat and listened to the sweet music.

Moments later, the vehicle slowed and made a turn onto a bumpy road. He parked and led me to a wall, where he turned my back to him.

"Wait here until I get you. And no peeking, young lady!" He was so serious that I couldn't help but laugh. I did as he instructed.

Keys rattled, and Slade cursed under his breath. My curiosity screamed to peek, but I waited until I was retrieved.

Cool air brushed my cheeks, and I took a deep breath. It was faint, but I caught the scent of wine, pastries, and spiced pot roast. I turned my head toward Slade. He put his hand on my face.

"Ready?" He asked.

"If that's food I smell, then yes!" I rubbed the silk covering my eyes.

He pulled off the blindfold. "Ta-da!" He gestured at the room.

My eyes adjusted, and I stared in speechless awe. It was a huge building with dim, sensual lighting. Streamers made with pink roses ran from ceiling to floor like vines. A candlelit meal sat on a round table in the center of the room. Against one of the walls was a vintage jukebox. There were a few people bustling around the edges of the room, and while three of them looked familiar, there was too much going on for me to make sense of any of it.

I turned to Slade, frowning in confusion. "What's—" He interrupted me with a long, deep kiss. He waved his arm at the room again, which was now suddenly devoid of people except for the two of us.

A sly grin stole over his face. "This, my dear Crisa, is how we play hooky."

Chapter 10

Slade

The amazement on Crisa's face brought a smile to mine. I had spent the morning calling in favors, cancelling appointments, and locating vacant, well-kept buildings to rent and arrange this special lunch date. At first, I worried I went over-the-top, but Crisa's expression removed any lingering doubts.

Crisa blinked.

"How did you ever manage something so extravagant?" she asked, eyes sparkling.

I shrugged. "It wasn't difficult, especially when it's to woo and win you," I said.

Crisa laughed. "Well, with me trapped in this abandoned building that's goodness-knows-how-far from civilization, do I get a say?"

"Not really," I said. I put my arm around her waist and pulled her close. "Not much at all."

"Well, Mr. Kidnapper, I must warn you that my boss is expecting me in less than an hour, and if I'm not on time, he might send a search party!"

I took a deep breath, and hoped for the best.

"Actually, ma'am, rumor has it that someone petitioned your boss for you to have the rest of the day off. Which means you're my hostage." Crisa's jaw dropped, and my chest tightened. I tried to keep my expression cool.

"Well," she sighed, her face unreadable, "I have a serious problem." She gestured around the large room, which was now empty except for the two of us.

"Problem?" I echoed.

She nodded. "I'm not sure if we should dance or eat first. I'm a little rusty on the etiquette of kidnappings." Her eyes met mine, and her serious expression dissolved. Dizzy with relief, I led her to the candlelit table. I wanted to sit to hide the way my knees trembled.

"Well, I've always heard it's rude to make a guest eat cold food, no matter what the occasion." I pulled out a seat for her, and then collapsed into mine with as much grace as I could manage.

"Even if that guest is your abductee?" she teased. I raised my eyebrows.

"Don't make me handcuff and gag you, madam," I murmured, sliding my chair closer to the table. She laughed again.

Crisa surveyed the spread that covered the table. She seemed impressed by the crisp white tablecloth, catered food and cheesy cloches I placed over the dishes to accent the rich ambiance. The wine had chilled to the perfect temperature, and I poured some into our glasses. Crisa lifted her head, and our eyes met.

"So, you never answered my question," she said.

"Which question was that?"

"How you managed to pull this off. There's no way you could've done this by yourself."

I paused, straightening a crooked knife so it was even with the fork. "Well, I asked friends in the office for help, and they were happy to lend a hand." She nodded, putting the clues together in her head.

"So, it's safe to assume that our secret romance is outta the bag?" She asked.

I should have discussed it with her first, since it involved information about her private life, as well as mine. I fumbled for an answer.

"That depends. Would you feel better if I told you everyone thought this was a business meeting?" I flashed a grin at my foolish question.

"I would feel better if we knew what this was first," she said. Her gentle tone persuaded me to meet her gaze, which penetrated the deepest part of my heart.

No longer hungry for food, I released her hands and clapped twice. On cue, the jukebox came to life, filling the room with the smooth chords of Michael Boston. I rose from my seat and offered my hand to Crisa, who took it, entranced.

I led her to the little dance floor and pulled her closer. We danced through the first two songs without a word.

Crisa broke the silence.

"Your heart is pounding like a drum," she said, breathless. I nestled my face in her hair, breathing in the scent of her lavender perfume.

"All the better to seduce you with, my dear," I replied. She turned her face up to mine, and her eyes burned in the dim candlelight. Enthralled, I leaned down and kissed her with all the heat and passion that roared in my body. Rather than pull away, she pressed herself against me. Her tongue found mine and swirled, sensual and needy. This wasn't how I intended the date to go, but I didn't want it to stop. I wasn't sure I *could* stop.

Crisa didn't keep me in suspense for long. She nibbled my lower lip and began to remove my tie. I sighed and pulled the hem of her soft blouse from the top of her skirt. My fingers caressed her stomach. Her skin quivered, and she pressed herself against me.

This was the point of no return, and it took everything in me to pause.

"Are you sure?" I asked, my voice thick and husky. She pulled my lips back to hers.

"Yes, Slade, please," she whimpered. "Please, make love to me."

I had no desire to deny her anything, and I bent to capture her lips again. This woman, who I was coming to believe was the love of my life, was asking me to make love to her, and I had every intent of delivering.

Chapter 11

Crisa

I lay next to Slade breathless, speechless at the incredible experience we had just shared. My emotions trembled as much as my muscles, and my tongue lay in knots, incapable of intelligent communication. I wanted to thank Slade, apologize to him for ever doubting him and beg him to come home with me, but all I could manage was a strange hiccup.

Slade's hand materialized on my cheek.

"Are you ok?" His voice shook with uncertainty. Giddiness overcame rational behavior, and I giggled like a schoolgirl.

"I think I saw Mars!" I announced. The childish outburst embarrassed me, but I couldn't stop. I peeked at Slade, ashamed.

To my relief, he started laughing with me.

"Just Mars? Damn, I gotta try harder next time. I was aiming for Saturn, at least!" He snorted.

I couldn't believe what was happening. Slade and I made the best love I'd ever known, on the floor of an empty building in the middle of who knew where, like high school kids. Now, we were laughing like 10-year-olds, and loving every minute of it! Could this be what it felt like with *the one?*

Insecurity gripped me as a light breeze wafted over me and I realized I was lying there naked. I reached for my blouse to cover myself, unsure what to think of my new, spur-of-the-moment behavior. Would this be a one-night stand for Slade now that we had sex? For once I wasn't trying to memorize the *Friends* pilot word-for-word while waiting for the man I was in bed with to leave, but what if he didn't feel the same?

Slade took my blouse with a gentle hand and moved it aside so he could examine my body with soft eyes. He stared for so long that I started to squirm.

"Beautiful," he whispered, then reached up and brushed my tousled hair from my face. His tone conveyed a million tiny tendernesses, and I moved closer to him and relaxed against his cool, damp chest. A secret smile crept to my lips, and I allowed it to stay.

I stroked his toned stomach with one finger as we relaxed in comfortable silence.

I opened my mouth but stopped, not sure what I wanted to say.

Slade's chest rumbled, and words started to flow. "Be my girlfriend."

His eyes locked on me, waiting for my response. Stunned, I sat up and searched his face for any indication that he was asking out of a sense of obligation or fickle love-drunkenness, but none existed. His hopeful expression made him appear boyish, and I giggled and kissed the top of his head. I thought of asking him for his varsity jacket, but thought it might not be best to keep teasing.

"How could I say no to that face?" I asked. He grinned.

"If my face is the only thing you can't say no to, I'm not doing this right," he growled and pinned me to the floor. Round two was shorter than round one, but twice as hot.

We left the empty building at sunset. My place was closer, so we stopped there for a shower to freshen up before deciding to see a movie. The plot had something to do with a girl who fell in love with a guy who dumped her best friend at the altar, but I spent too much time sneaking glances at Slade to pay attention. He wanted to call me his girlfriend and now

I could say I have a boyfriend. My tummy did a little flip. How would my kids accept the news? Afterward, we stopped at a ritzy bar.

In the middle of a cheesy joke, Slade's phone rang. The first two times, he pressed ignore without missing a word of our conversation. When the caller persisted, I encouraged him to answer.

"It might be that jealous wife of yours," I teased. He made a sarcastic face and stepped outside to take the call.

When Slade returned, he had no color on his face. He sat by me without a word, his expression grim and hands trembling. I rubbed his arm and waited until he was ready to tell me what happened. The bartender gave a nod, as if asking if something was needed. Slade motioned for another drink; whatever the news, it wasn't good.

He downed half his drink when the bartender brought it and took a ragged breath.

"That was my aunt in Michigan," he began. His dull, flat voice contrasted against the emotions that stormed in his eyes. "My grandfather— He's been sick for a couple of months. We thought he was going to pull through, but—" He cleared his throat. "He passed away earlier this evening."

I covered his hand with my own and squeezed gently. My heart ached for him.

Slade shook his head and offered me a tight smile.

"Frowns give you wrinkles," he said as he tore the napkin he held in half.

The weakness of his joke brought a sting to my eyes. I kissed his shoulder to hide them. "When's the funeral?" I asked.

"Day after tomorrow. I booked the first flight out, which isn't until tomorrow morning. I'm gonna pack a bag and then get to the airport in case something earlier opens up."

I nodded. "I'll wait with you if you want." I expected him to refuse, but he shot me a pale but genuine smile.

"You're an angel," he said.

Chapter 12

Slade

The news of my grandfather's death shook me. I clung to Crisa's calm demeanor and words of comfort. She stayed collected and rational, and I bit my tongue to keep from asking her to marry me right then and there.

For 9 p.m. on a weekday, there wasn't much activity at the airport. I registered my duffel bag as carry-on luggage, and led Crisa to a seat between the ticket desk and the flight board. The terrible elevator music that drifted from invisible speakers created a jarring cacophony of sound combined with the live news feed and sports channels playing on the two televisions above where Crisa and I sat.

Crisa picked up a magazine and leafed through it, but I noticed she wasn't really looking at the pages. It

seemed selfish to drag her along. I knew she'd rather
be at home with a good book, or pulling out all of her
teeth, than waiting all night in an airport with her sad
sack of a boyfriend.

I decided I wouldn't put her through the
insufferable wait.

"Let me put you in a cab, so you can go," I said. I
pulled out my cell phone and started to autodial the
cab company I frequently used.

She frowned. "Am I making you uncomfortable? I
can put away the magazine if the page flipping is
bothering you."

I blinked, surprised.

"Not at all, darlin'. You being here with me is all
that's keeping me going right now, if I'm honest. I
just hate the idea of you sitting here exhausted and
bored silly. You should go home and get some rest."

She smiled. I'd never experienced so much care
and concern in one evening, let alone one
relationship.

"There's nowhere else I'd rather be. I wouldn't be
able to rest, knowing you're here alone," she said.

"You're the sweetest woman I've ever met." I took
her hand in mine and squeezed it gratefully.

"Then quit trying to get rid of me," she replied.

Neither of us said much after that. The loud ding
of an intercom jerked me from an awkward doze a

while later. I looked at Crisa, afraid I'd disturbed her reading, but she was asleep against my shoulder. Her hair draped across her lovely face. I resisted the urge to tuck it behind her ear. I couldn't bring myself to disturb her and contented myself with thoughts of how lucky I was to have found her after all these years of dating.

I waited as long as I could, but when I glanced at the clock on the wall and saw my flight was due to leave in an hour, I nudged Crisa. She blinked awake and gave me a sleepy smile as she stretched. We walked as far as the airport security rules allowed, and I took her in my arms when we reached the checkpoint.

"I'll call as soon as the plane lands." I gave her a peck on the lips.

"I hope to hear from you, but I know things might be hectic. I completely understand if you aren't able to call or text until things settle down."

I reluctantly let go of her. "Thanks again for keeping me company." I brought her face to mine and gave her a sweet, lingering kiss. At last, I released her from my grip.

"I should be gone for three or four days, but I'll let you know whatever happens."

She nodded again and stroked my chin, five-o'clock shadow and all.

"Have a safe trip."

I nodded, and her hand trailed down my arm and then down to the tips of my fingers. She held on until we were forced to part as I headed through security. When I was through, I looked back, seeking one final glimpse of her. She was still standing where I'd left her, the first rays of the sunrise beaming through the airport windows and surrounding her in an ethereal glow. I raised my hand to wave one last time, and she waved back as I turned and headed to my plane.

The funeral for my grandfather was nice, but modest. His retirement hadn't afforded him wealth, but it kept life comfortable for him and my grandmother. The will wasn't read until two days after the service, so I stayed longer than planned. My grandfather didn't leave much for his relatives to inherit, but we all attended the reading as a legal formality. I booked a flight home the following day.

It was wonderful to see my family, but I was anxious to get back to my usual life and more importantly, back to Crisa. I was due to land at 4:15 p.m., so I made plans for a grand surprise date for Crisa. She thought I'd be landing later, which allowed me to arrange a limo to pick her up from work. I got us in on a romantic cruise around the bay. Whether we made love was irrelevant to me. What I wanted was to create the perfect celebration of our new relationship, and confess I was in love with her.

My plane landed fifteen minutes behind schedule, and I flagged a cab and begged the driver to rush to the office as fast as possible to make sure the limo driver wouldn't miss Crisa on her way out of the building. I planned to greet Crisa at the dock entrance with a huge bouquet of red roses. It was an uneventful drive; we arrived at the office within 20 minutes, and I instructed the driver to park beside a delivery van where I'd have a clear view of the exit door and limo. Minutes passed like hours, but at last she emerged, more beautiful than I remembered.

She laughed, and I saw she was walking with someone in a trench coat. I kicked myself for being inconsiderate. What if she had other plans? My breath caught as I recognized the man. It was one of Harrison's new interns. He said something to Crisa, causing her to laugh again. I waited for Crisa to split from him and head toward her car, but instead they stopped walking and faced one another. When Crisa stepped forward and kissed the guy, it took a second for me to comprehend what I was witnessing.

The man was taller than me, so Crisa stretched up on tiptoe in order to kiss him. He put his hand on her waist and rested her arm on his. I watched in shock, unable to move or speak. Crisa broke the kiss after

several agonizing seconds. She waved to him and headed toward the parking lot. She never saw the limo.

The limo driver eased toward her, and the movement broke my paralysis. I grabbed my cell phone and told him to cancel the pickup. I couldn't go through with the date, and I wasn't ready to confront her about what I saw.

Without a word, the taxi driver started the cab and drove out of the parking lot, careful to avoid Crisa as we left. I pointed to a liquor store a mile from my house.

"Let me off there." The taxi rolled to a stop. I needed fresh air and a stiff drink.

"Sorry," I mumbled. I tossed a handful of twenties on the seat and slammed the door. The walk home offered little comfort, but I came to a clear, though painful, decision: I could no longer be with Crisa. If our relationship meant so little to her that she was kissing other men while I was at a funeral, then we had no future together. All that was left now was to tell her.

Chapter 13

Crisa

S lade had been gone less than a week, but to me it felt like a lifetime. My days revolved around his texts and phone calls; I couldn't sleep until we talked each night. By the time 4:30 p.m. on the day he was coming back rolled around, I could barely contain myself while I waited for his plane to arrive.

I gathered my things and prepared to fly through the office lobby and out the front door, but I heard someone call my name. I saw Jack Bearson, a new intern, leaning against a pillar in front of the elevators. I'd had lunch with Jack earlier in the week. He wanted to pick my brain about the company and any processes I could share. He wanted to learn how

to be more efficient. I had a wonderful time. He was funny and charismatic, and I enjoyed his company.

"Hi!" I said, breathless then pushed the P for the parking garage.

"Where's the fire?" Jack teased.

"Slade's coming home tonight, and I have errands to run before meeting him at the airport."

"Well, let me walk you to your car so you don't hurry yourself into an unscheduled meeting with the pavement. The door dinged, then opened. Jack held the door letting me enter first.

Despite my wild nerves at Slade's return, I laughed at his joke.

"I'd like to see that! Let me know when people have scheduled meetings with the pavement!" My mouth twisted in amusement.

"I heard the first one is scheduled for November 31."

I caught the joke as we stepped out of the elevator, and I laughed so loud that several people stared at us.

"Is that before or after Leap Year?" I asked.

He thought for a moment.

"Add a Leap Year, carry Valentine's Day, and divide by Friday the 13th." Jack began to laugh with me.

We stopped so I could catch my breath. He turned to face me.

"I forgot to thank you for lunch the other day. I had a wonderful time," I said.

"It was my pleasure," he said. "Really. It was nice learning about the company's history."

The air around us hummed. I enjoyed being around Jack— he'd be a good catch for any woman. A question popped into my head as I looked and listened to Jack. I was certain that what Slade and I had was special, but maybe that spark wasn't as uncommon as I once thought. Was there really such a thing as magic between people? Could I trust my judgment when it's always led me astray in the past?

There was only one way to know for sure. I impulsively rolled onto the balls of my feet and leaned up to kiss Jack. His lips were warm and soft, but the zing, the magic that made Slade's kisses exceptional, wasn't there. It took effort to contain my sigh of relief. Jack must have noticed the lack of electricity, because he broke the kiss.

"With a 'thank you' like that, I'll take you to lunch every day," he said jokingly. "See you around the office?"

I laughed, embarrassed. Mortified, I then covered my mouth, "Jack? I—I—Oh, I'm so sorry. I don't know what came over me." My voice cracked, so I sucked air deep into my lungs. "You know I'm seeing Slade."

Jack gave me a lopsided grin.

"It's okay. I understand more than you know. I have three sisters. Slade is a lucky man. Now go get your errands done. Give him the welcome home you've been planning."

I eyed my car, then waved goodbye, anxious to get out of there and get ready for my evening with Slade.

The quiet drive to the airport had me thinking about my behavior. Shame coursed through my veins. I expected more from myself after having to deal with a cheating husband. It wasn't fair to Slade that I would violate his trust. He certainly deserved better. Our relationship needed to stay honest. *I'll tell Slade what happened and ask for his forgiveness.*

I didn't realize Slade's plane was late until I awoke in my seat at 6:45 p.m. at the airport. I wanted to meet him at the baggage claim area, but I must have dozed off while I waited. The flight boards showed no delays or cancellations when I scanned them, so I headed through the crowd to an information desk. After a seven-minute wait in line, the attendant told me Slade's flight had arrived that afternoon, hours before he told me to expect him.

Confused, I staggered from the desk. Did he have a surprise planned? I was sure he wasn't avoiding me, but maybe I ruined things by being here instead of at home. I checked my phone. There wasn't a single text or missed call from Slade. His cell number went straight to voice-mail three times in a row. Confusion turned to concern when I called his work extension and his house phone with no success. If he went to my house to find me, his cell might have died, which would at least explain why he wasn't home. With renewed hope, I drove home as fast as I could, but there was no sign of his car or him.

As I stepped inside the house the phone rang. I raced to answer before the caller hung up. The machine caught it first, and I recognized Slade's voice.

"Hello, Slade? Hi, I'm here!" I answered, relieved. "Are you ok?"

"We need to talk," he said. The muffled stiffness of his voice made it hard to understand him.

"What's wrong? Did something happen while you were gone?"

No answer.

"Slade? Hello?"

"Crisa, just listen, okay?" He growled. I tried to stay calm.

"Of course. What is it?"

"I think we should see other people," he said. I opened my mouth, but no sound came out. The room tilted on its axis as his words sunk in.

"I just don't think you and I can ever work in the real world."

I wasn't aware that what we were was make-believe! My thoughts worked, but my lips didn't.

He sighed.

"I realized while I was gone that we don't have a real, tangible future together. I mean, the idea of us is damn near perfect, but—" He paused. I found my voice at last.

"While you were gone?" I shouted. I hadn't meant to raise my voice. Slade inhaled sharply. "Was this before or after you called me every night, telling me how much you missed me?" I tried to rein in my emotions, but all the anger and betrayal I felt toward Alan for his infidelity rushed to greet this new, raw pain. "Or did some floozy show you what you'd be missing in the airplane bathroom on your flight back?"

"Crisa, that's not fair," he said.

I snorted. "You wanna talk about unfair? How fair was it when you staged an elaborate lunch and dancing to lure me into screwing you on the floor of an empty building? How is it fair that, twenty-four hours ago, you said you couldn't wait to be with me again, and now you find words to hurt me?"

"I'm not doing this to hurt you, Crisa," he said.

Despite the situation, I laughed. "Of course not. In fact, I guess this should feel pretty damn good, right? In that case, thank you so much. I sure had the whole dating thing backwards. Thank you for coming along and clearing things up for me."

I hung up without another word. I'd wasted enough breath and time on Slade. It looked like I had been right to compare him to Alan, after all. Even though I was foolish enough to fall in love with him, at least I hadn't been crazy enough to tell him. The thought brought me no solace, and I buried my face in my hands and began to sob.

Chapter 14

Slade

Crisa took the breakup harder than I expected, considering she'd replaced me before the relationship even ended. I couldn't believe she would be capable of something as heartbreaking as cheating. *I guess you can never really know someone.* Crisa's infidelity was the very reason I remained single. If women weren't insane, psycho stalkers like Rebecca, they were either gold diggers or cheaters or both. This solidified my resolve to stay single. It would be a very long time before I considered attempting to date again.

I turned on my cell phone and checked the messages on my home phone. I saw how many times Crisa had tried calling. It surprised me that she had tried so hard to reach me since she had her new

boyfriend to keep her busy. *Maybe she was trying to break things off.* No, that couldn't be it. She was too upset when I broke the news to her. None of it made sense, but I was too exhausted to try. I hoped she wasn't going to be both a cheater and a nut job. Then again, it might be a refreshing change from Rebecca's old-fashioned crazy.

I turned off my house phone ringer and powered down my cell phone again. Satisfied that nobody would bother me, I grabbed a bottle of bourbon from my liquor cabinet, ignoring the club soda I bought at the store, and took a long drink straight from the bottle. It burned going down, but the fire dulled the hollow feeling in my chest. Bringing the bourbon with me, I dragged myself to the den and flopped onto the couch. I turned on the television, not really paying attention to what was playing. I just needed something dull and mindless to distract me until the bourbon lulled me into an alcohol-induced sleep.

Harrison had given me the entire week off of work because of my grandfather's death. When I awoke at noon the next day with the worst hangover and neck crick I'd had in years, I was grateful. I stumbled into the bathroom and choked down three aspirin from the medicine cabinet. They didn't stay down long, but luckily, I was standing by the toilet. After my stomach rejected everything I had consumed the day before, I took a shower. The cool water soothed my throbbing head and washed away the sticky alcohol-tinged sweat that clung to my skin. My stomach settled considerably once I was clean and dressed, so I made myself plain, dry toast, hoping to end what was left of the awful hangover.

Once I felt better, I checked my voicemail boxes, expecting both to be full of messages from Crisa. However, both were empty. In fact, she hadn't tried to call me once. For a moment I almost forgot about the events of the day before and I picked up the phone to call her, concerned that something was wrong. The memories flooded back in a rush, and I hung up before it could ring. I chuckled out loud at myself, then ambled to my study. Since I felt a little less crappy and needed to keep my mind busy, I tried to do a little work at home.

I spent the afternoon answering client emails and scheduling consultations for the next week. Around 6 p.m. I shut down my computer and ordered takeout from a small Chinese restaurant a couple of blocks away. I opted to pick up the food rather than having it delivered. The cool evening breeze relieved some tension. By the time I made it back home, I felt almost like my old self.

The phone was ringing when I entered, but I studiously ignored it, sure it was Crisa calling again.

As I was arranging the food cartons on the dining table, the phone rang again. The answering machine beeped, and a man's voice echoed through the speaker.

"Hey there young man, it's Nel. My wife and I are having a small party on our yacht this weekend. I thought I'd give you a ring and see if you wanted—"

I abandoned the food and rushed to grab the phone before he hung up. Nel was an old college friend, and though he was barely two years older than me, he got a big kick out of calling me "young man" or "kid." I hadn't seen him in over a year and was glad he called.

"Nel? Hey, you still there?" I answered. He chuckled.

"Hey, kiddo. I was beginning to think you were out on a hot date." I shuddered.

"Not even close, my friend," I replied, barely containing the bitterness in my voice.

"Lady troubles?" He asked.

"More of the usual," I said. I wasn't quite ready to talk about what had happened with Crisa, so I changed the subject. "So, what's this about a yacht party?"

"Yes sir. Sue and I are throwing a little party on Saturday. She's retiring from teaching this week, and we wanted to do a little something to celebrate."

"Retiring?" Sue was a year younger than me. It seemed a little early for her to be retiring.

"Yeah. Her mom caught pneumonia this past winter and almost died. So Sue took a leave from work for nearly two months to help care for her mother. When she returned home, she realized that neither of her parents were in very good health. With early retirement she'd be available to visit and help them as needed."

"Oh, bless her heart," I said. I thought of my grandfather, and my heart went out to Sue. "Sure, I'd love to come to the party. Tell Sue I'll definitely be there, and congratulations on the early retirement."

"Will do," Nel said. "Oh, and don't worry about dressing to impress. It's supposed to be 80 degrees this weekend, so it's a casual thing."

"Got it," I said, "and thanks for the invitation. I'm glad you called."

"See you Saturday, kid." We said our goodbyes, and I hung up the phone.

I returned to my now-cold food, but I didn't mind. Nel's call and invitation had been what I needed to boost my mood. I was halfway through dinner when a pain hit me in the chest. At first, I thought it was indigestion. I took a couple of antacids and attempted to finish eating. The second chest pain lasted longer and moved down my left arm. My chest suddenly felt

as if an elephant was using it for a chair. It became difficult to breathe, and the realization hit me like a freight train: I was having a heart attack.

I tried to stand and get to the phone, but I could barely move. I crawled across the kitchen floor. For a moment, I considered using my cell phone to call 911, but I knew my landline would help dispatch locate me if the call was disconnected or I lost consciousness before I could give them the address. The last thing I was conscious of was the phone falling to the floor as I knocked it out of its cradle and dialed the numbers with numb fingers. Then, everything went black.

Chapter 15

Crisa

I called in sick to work the day after Slade's cruel breakup. In truth, I didn't plan to return to work at the office. It was bad enough to break up with someone you work with, but the entire firm knew about us and it would only be a matter of time before they found out about this, too. I didn't have an explanation to offer. *I don't know what happened— He went out of town, and when he came back, he didn't want me anymore.* That sounded childish and lame, even to me. I shook my head, losing all control. With trembling fingers, I brushed away the tears that fell down my cheeks.

I took a long, hot shower and scrubbed my skin raw, hoping to cleanse myself of the shame I felt. I couldn't believe I let myself think Slade was different

than any other man. They all wanted one thing. Once they got it, they would say and do anything to get rid of you. I thought again about Alan's indiscretions. A wave of sadness, anger, and grief swept me away, and I collapsed, sobbing, onto the shower floor. I cried for the pain Alan's unfaithful trysts had caused me. I cried because of all the horrible dates and meaningless sex I'd had while trying to cope with that pain. I cried because, despite everything, I missed Alan. I missed his companionship, and the warmth of his body heat while we slept. But, most of all, I cried because I really had fallen in love with Slade, and he broke my heart. Just like Alan.

I crawled out of the shower and wrapped a towel around my naked body. I caught a glimpse of my reflection in the mirror above my bathroom sink, and I almost laughed. *Look at yourself. Let another man break your heart, and then whine like a baby about it.*

"There, art thou happy?" I said aloud to my reflection to break the silence and regain some composure. I might have been hurt, but I'd be damned if I was going to sit around crying into a pint of ice cream like a teenager. Men. It would likely be another bad decision. Time to focus on a hobby, or something I can do. At least those choices won't break my heart like Alan and now Slade.

As I was getting dressed, the phone rang. I ran into my bedroom and grabbed the cordless I kept beside the bed. For a second, I hesitated. The caller ID said it was the office. *What if it's Slade?* Finally, I answered.

"Hello?" I said, my voice sharp.

"Crisa?" Harrison's voice resonated in my ear. *Oh no, he already knows!*

"Y-yes, Mr. Harrison? What can I do for you?" I tried to keep my voice calm and cool.

"I'm sorry to call you at home, especially with you not feeling well, but I'm afraid I have some bad news."

"What's wrong, Mr. Harrison?"

"Slade's sister, Kelly, just called. Slade had a heart attack. He's been rushed to St. Lucy's hospital. They don't know yet how serious it is, but he was unconscious when the paramedics arrived." I fell onto the bed. My previous anger toward Slade vanished. I felt numb.

"A heart attack?" I echoed.

"Yes," Harrison said. "I called you because Slade's sister didn't have your number, and she said, in his brief moments of consciousness, he has been asking for you." I opened my mouth to respond, but nothing came out.

"Crisa? Are you still there?" Harrison asked. I cleared my throat.

"Yes, I'm sorry sir. I'm just—in shock." *For more than one reason,* I added silently.

"I know. We all are. Again, I'm sorry for calling you like this, but I wanted to make sure someone got in contact with you. I know he cares a great deal about you." I was speechless, but I managed to stammer a thank you to Harrison before I hung up.

I sat staring at the phone in my hand for what felt like hours. I had a decision to make. There was no way of knowing whether Slade really wanted there, or if he'd just temporarily forgotten our breakup. It didn't matter. In my mind, I didn't *have* a choice. I had to go to him.

Slade's sister was in the cardiology floor's waiting room when I arrived at the hospital. She heard me give my name to the nurse behind the information desk and rushed over to greet me.

"I'm so glad you made it!" she said, shaking my hand.

"I'm sorry, how rude of me! I'm Kelly, Slade's sister." I returned her handshake and murmured a greeting.

"His room is down this hall. Follow me I'll take you to him. They're only letting visitors see him for a few minutes at a time," she told me. I nodded.

We walked to his room in silence. When we reached his door, Kelly rubbed my arm and offered me a small smile before she headed back to the waiting room. I took a deep breath and stepped inside.

Slade looked weak and helpless. His skin was pale and ashen. He was hooked up to several machines, and tubes and cords were everywhere. His eyelids looked bruised. I moved quietly to his bedside and took his hand, which was cold.

"Slade?" I whispered, gently rubbing the top of his hand with my thumb. I didn't expect a response, since Harrison had told me he was in and out of consciousness. To my surprise, he stirred. His hand gave mine a weak squeeze, and his eyes fluttered.

"Kelly said you were asking for me," I said, feeling dumb. What if he didn't really want me here, and I was upsetting him? I started to drop his hand and run, but he gripped it tighter. His eyes finally opened and he looked at me.

"Crisa?" he muttered. He smiled weakly.

"Yeah. I'm here," I said. His voice was soft, so I had to lean in to hear him.

"I'm— I'm sorry," he said.

"For what?" I asked, although I thought I knew.

"I saw you—saw you kiss that Jack guy. I was hurt—" His voice trailed as he started to doze. My heart sank. *So* that's *why he broke up with me.* The

realization of what he must have thought hit me full force. I felt terrible. Every mean thought I'd had about Slade flashed through my mind, and I nearly started crying when I realized that it had been my fault the whole time.

"Oh Slade, I'm— I'm so sorry! He's a friend! He took me to lunch one day at work, and I thought..." *What had I been thinking? That's just it, I wasn't. How foolish!* "Forget what I thought. It was a mistake. An experiment of sorts, to see if there was magic." I leaned in and nuzzled his cheek. My voice quaked with tears. "I'm in love with you," I whispered. "I'm so sorry!" Slade's eyes were closed again. Realizing the doctor must have left orders to medicate him and keep him calm and out of pain, it occurred to me that he might not even remember this conversation when he was conscious again. I thought for a second time about leaving, but he spoke again.

"No, Crisa, I'm sorry." His voice became stronger. "I should have talked to you. Instead I dumped you like some high school kid. You deserved better."

"I don't blame you, Slade! Hell, if our positions were reversed, I would have thought—and probably done, exactly what you did!" He blinked, and his eyes started to shimmer.

"I was an idiot. Forgive me?" Despite the lump in my throat, I laughed.

"Forgive you? The better question is: can *you* forgive *me*?" I asked. He reached for me with his other hand, which had a large I.V. needle taped to the back of his hand. I gently held onto his fingertips to avoid bumping it.

"Nothing to forgive," he said. "You coming here to be with me, after what I did to you, tells me how wrong I was. I'll never forgive myself for overreacting." His voice thickened, but it wasn't because of the medicine this time. I rubbed his hands and gently shushed him.

"Relax, you're going to work yourself into a tizzy," I chastised. "Of course I forgive you, and I'll be right here for as long as you want me." I meant every word as I spoke. He studied me for a long moment, then relaxed against the bed. His eyes began to droop again, and I released one of his hands and grabbed the chair near the head of his bed, pulling it as close as I could. I sat holding the hand without the I.V. If I ignored the machines, a comfortable silence filled the room. For a while, I thought he was asleep. He startled me when he broke the calm.

"Crisa?" He said. His voice was tentative, but no longer retained its sedated sluggishness.

"Yes, sweetheart, I'm here," I said.

"Marry me."

My jaw dropped. Certain it was the drugs talking, I kissed the back of his hand and shook my head.

"Let's get you well and back home first, hun." I bit my lip, not sure if it was the meds talking.

He lifted his head a fraction. "I'm serious." He must have read the look on my face. "I know I'm higher than summertime kites, but I know what I'm saying. I love you, Crisa. Please say yes."

I sat, shocked, for a moment. I expected Slade to drift off to sleep, but his eyes were alert and focused intently on me. At last, I took a long, deep breath.

"Yes, Slade," I said. "Yes, I'll marry you!"

He sagged against his pillows, relief washing across his face as he gave me a brilliant smile. "I want nothing more than to spend the rest of my life with you, Crisa, and I couldn't bear it if I let the chance to call you my wife slip away."

I leaned in and kissed him gently, pouring all of my love and joy into the sweet press of my lips against his. "I know the feeling," I murmured as I pulled away. I dropped another kiss on the side of his head and settled back into my chair. "Now go to sleep. You need your rest if you're going to be well enough to carry me across the threshold on our wedding day."

He winked at me and gestured at himself. "Don't let the tubes fool you, sweetheart; I'm stronger than I look."

I shook my head in amusement at his antics and squeezed his hand as he began to drift off. When his breathing evened out into the slow rhythm of sleep, I felt tears well in my eyes once again- only this time, they were tears of happiness. I couldn't believe how close I had come to losing this incredible man, and I was thankful beyond measure that I had gotten a second chance. There was no one I would rather wake up with in the morning and fall asleep curled up against at night, and I planned to make sure he knew exactly how much I loved him for the rest of our lives.

The End

Diana Lynn

Since she was a child, Diana wanted to be a writer.
But her dreams were sidelined as life had other plans.
Then one day she signed up for a writing course and
wrote what she liked to read – Romance, Fantasy, and
Women's Fiction. She began writing her first
women's fiction where the couple worked through
their troubles. You have to stay positive, and when
something doesn't work, find a way to make it work.

Diana enjoys creating, whether it's sewing, painting,
designing, or creating other types of books. She's
created several coloring books and journals. Diana
believes We are all dreamers and Everyone deserves a
rainbow.

Final Words

Final words from the author…

Hope you've enjoyed this novel.

It was my utmost privilege plotting and writing this novel for you to enjoy.

It'll help get the word out so more people can enjoy this book and it will help me out a lot. I would greatly appreciate it. Thank you.

Sincerely,

Diana Lynn

Ways to reach her:

Email: diana@dianalynn.com

Facebook: facebook.com/dianalynn

Website: https://www.dianalynn.com

Visit her Amazon Author Page and see her other published books: